windy
souls
Jonah Lang

I dedicate this book to my family

 tredition

© 2023 Jonah Lang
Coverdesign von: Jonah Lang

Druck und Distribution im Auftrag des Autors:
tredition GmbH, Heinz-Beusen-Stieg 5, 22926 Ahrensburg, Germany

hello my friend, long time ago i last heard from you. How are you ? i recognized that you don't come around often anymore. Not that it bothers me, don't get me wrong, you know what i mean.

oh hey, i honestly wouldn't have expected to see you this soon after our last talk. Is this a coincidence? You don't took this tram road with me in a long time. Like i said don't get me wrong but it would be nice of you to leave the tram at the next stop.

are you serious? I told you before you're not allowed to visit me at work. I need my space here and i don't want you to be seen by my coworkers. I could get in trouble, please leave me alone.

okay, now it's getting creepy, have you been here the whole night? I can imagine more beautiful things than waking up next to you. I mean i accept the fact that you are coming more often again but let me have my morning for myself. See you later.

dude, you're too pushy now. Are you gonna leave at some point? Don't you get it ? there is not enough space for the both of us.
I already avoid my friends because I don't want them to see you. Please give me time to breath.

are you following me? I've never showed you this place. How did you find me?
You're lucky that i'm alone. You are and you will be my secret. Why do you want to be seen?

it wouldn't end well for the both of us.

do you know what? I try to don't be upset anymore. I obviously don't get rid of you. You are a part of me, I have to accept you fear.

J.

I feel separated from myself
I don't know who I am anymore
The room is full of light
But when I look in the mirror
Everything is pitch dark
I try to light it up
But my lighter runs out of gas

J.

I wake up at night
Screaming
Sweating
And once again I ask myself
„Will this ever stop"

J.

I thought you were different
I trusted you
But as it always happens
You disappeared out of my life
And what once was hope
Is now bitter disappointment

J.

I always blamed you
But it wasn't your fault
You did not break me
I let myself get broken by you

J.

And when the sun went down
I knew you wouldn't be home
I always knew it
Because you aren't real
And you probably never will be
And that's the hardest thing to realize

J.

What if I never knew you
Sometimes im not sure if it was all in my head
Our so called „love"
It wasn't our reality
Yet I could have pretended the real love was there
But I never got this from you

J.

I feel like I'm always standing on a rope
One word
One sentence
One look
And I'll fall down

J.

I feel like I'm standing on a street
People and cars rushing by
And I'm in the middle
Crying and screaming
But the noise around me is to loud
Nobody hears me
Thousands of people are there
But also no one
Will I be seen
Before I dissolve?

J.

Laying in your bed all by yourself
Wishing to have someone beside you
Who holds you and comforts you
But not being able to have someone
Because you don't have the strength
To get to know each other

J.

At first it wasn't more than a thought
Now it's not much more
Not even a chance
Although you finally recognized me

J.

Those pills give me feelings
Feelings no human could ever give me
They make things bearable
They make me go outside
They saved my life
Yet they also took everything

J.

Feeling your skin on mine
While we both try to remember the love we once felt
And trying to enjoy it while it lasts
Because we both know
The emptiness inside comes after

J.

The first time i saw that smile
That wonderful genuine smile
Your eyes were the purest thing i've ever seen
I imagined getting lost for hours

J.

When I opened my eyes
You leaned forward and kissed me
The touch of your lips on mine
Was everything I needed that morning

J.

sometimes i like to think we would meet in a record store. i'm holding „louder than bombs" in my hands. i imagine you asking me if it's the last one. i'll tell you that it is but that you can have it if you like. i give it to you and you ask me if i would like to listen to it together. it becomes our thing. we show each other our record collections, listen and talk about them. we start to like each other. after some time we listen to „louder than bombs" again. we come to the point where the song „asleep" comes on.

i tell you how the song saved my life. all the pain i've went through, that im not an easy person to be in a relationship with. i tell you that i'm afraid to hurt you. you tell me about your favorite book „the fault in our stars" and that the main character says „you don't get to choose if you get hurt in this world, but you do have a say in who hurts you". i look at you with tears in my eyes while you lean over and start to kiss me. i tell you that this is what i wanted all my life and you reply „i was always here waiting for you"

J.

I miss the feeling of falling in love
Maybe if you hold my hand
We can feel it for just a second

J.

Honest dating bio:

in order to get a match, you need to write a few sentences about yourself:

a few sentences.. okay this will be not easy. maybe it's easier if i just tell you about my typical day. not long after i wake up i usually make myself coffee first. i'm not very hungry in the morning so i often eat breakfast not until noon. until then i often read or watch something on the tv. after my „breakfast" i take a walk with my dog and enjoy the fresh air. in the afternoon i like to paint just whatever comes to my mind. i love to cook.. actually that's what i'm doing right now so i think i will finish writing this tomorrow..

you know today i had a different day. in fact everything i wrote yesterday is only half true. i mean my day does look like this sometimes, but often it doesn't. i figured that i want to be honest because it's a part of me. i know that it can be fun having me around but you need to know that it's not all the time. there are days like today where i can barely move. i can't leave my bed, can't use my phone, can't even watch netflix because it's too exhausting. I can't answer texts, pick up the phone, even talking is hard sometimes. I wish i could say that was all. It's hard for me to trust someone and have very strong fear of abandonment, which makes it hard to be in a relationship with me. i know sounds like a dream right? but doesn't everybody deserve to be loved?

but that's what's it's all about right? love. i don't want to hide my real me, i'm working on getting better but it probably won't go away completely. i would write more but i'm running out of letters.
so if this doesn't scare you off leave me message, i can't wait to meet you.
xx Jonah

I wanna get lost in somebody's eyes again

J.

Its a beautiful thought
That the universe has a love story planned for me
Its a thought I believe in truly
Just like in the movies

J.

As the water starts to rise
I can feel it as well in my eyes
The ignorance starts to prevail
We can see it everyday on every scale
Why do I feel so helpless
It seems like we are meant to fail

J.

Thank you for supporting me.

About the Author

Jonah Lang, born in 1997, discovered that he can express a lot of feelings through his writing. It always helped him to deal with different emotions and reflect himself. With this short book he wants to publish a few of his most meaningful poems.

Zeitfracht Medien GmbH
Ferdinand-Jühlke-Straße 7
99095 Erfurt, Deutschland
produktsicherheit@kolibri360.de